Pony Surprise

Adapted by Meredith Rusu

from the teleplay by
Grant Moran

Scholastic Inc.

americangirl.com/service

ISBN 978-1-338-32590-4

10 9 8 7 6 5 4 3 2 1   19 20 21 22 23

Printed in the U.S.A   40
First printing 2019

Book design by Carolyn Bull
Animation art direction by Jessica Rogers and Riley Wilkinson

Scholastic Inc.
557 Broadway, New York, NY 10012

The WellieWishers are playing in the garden one afternoon when Camille spots a shimmering surprise. "Guys, come and see this!" she calls to her friends. "The fairies have left us a wishing well!"

Willa, Emerson, Ashlyn, and Kendall rush over. A big pool of rainwater has filled a hollow tree stump in the garden. Camille is right—it must be a magical wishing well!

"Let's make a wish right now!" Emerson says.

"But you can't make a wish without a coin," Ashlyn points out.

"You mean like *this* coin?" Emerson pulls out a shiny gold coin—exactly what they need to make a wish!

"That's perfect!" cheer her friends. "What should we wish for?"
"How about wings, so we can fly?" suggests Willa.
"Or rocket-powered roller skates, so we can go super fast," adds Kendall.
But Emerson thinks she has the best idea of all. "Let's wish for a pony!"

"Hold it, you guys!" Camille suddenly says. "We can't make any wish yet."

"Why not?" asks Emerson. "I've got the coin. We're all ready. Let's do it!"

"Because we only get *one* wish," Camille explains. "So we all have to agree, and we all have to do it together."

"Oh," says Emerson.

"*And*," says Camille, "we need to have a wishing ceremony to make the fairies happy."

"A wishing ceremony?" Emerson moans. "That will take forever!"

"You can *never* rush fairies," Camille says. "Will everyone help with the ceremony?"

"We will," say Willa, Ashlyn, and Kendall.

"Okay, fine," Emerson agrees. "As long as it doesn't take *too* long."

Camille gives everyone a job to do to prepare for a wishing ceremony.

Ashlyn finds fairy wings for them all to wear.

Willa chooses colorful flowers to decorate the well.

Kendall collects stones to mark the wishing circle.
And Camille picks reeds so they can play a magical tune.

Back by the wishing well, Emerson is in charge of making up a fairy dance. But her heart isn't in it.

"This is taking so long!" she groans. "I don't understand why we have to do a whole ceremony. I wish we could make our wish right now!"

Suddenly, Emerson looks around. Her friends are all far away. None of them would see if she secretly tossed the coin into the well and made a wish.

"It is *my* coin," Emerson says. "And everyone would love a pony."

Emerson can't help herself. "I'm going to do it! I wish for a pony!"

Plop! Emerson's coin splashes into the water.

Clip clop! The sound of hooves trot up behind her.

Emerson gasps. She turns around and comes face-to-face with . . . a pony.

A real pony!

"Oh my gosh," Emerson cries. "I *got* my wish! I got my wish!"

Then, she stops. "Oh no. I got *my* wish. What will the others say when they realize I didn't wait for them?"

Emerson feels guilty. "I have to hide this pony before they get back!"

Quickly, she tries to lead the pony to a nearby field. But it breaks away and heads for the garden instead.

"No!" Emerson pleads. "Not that way!"

Clip clop, clip clop. The pony trots right over to Ashlyn.

Thinking fast, Emerson nudges the pony into their playhouse and out of sight. "Phew, that was close!"

But Emerson's problems aren't over. The pony sneaks out the back of the playhouse and heads toward the other WellieWishers.

It prances past Camille.

It trots behind Kendall.

It even tries to nibble some of Willa's flowers!

Luckily, the girls are too busy to notice the pony, but Emerson is really worried now.

That silly pony just won't stay hidden!

"What am I going to do?" Emerson wails.

Just then, she hears her friends coming over. She frantically throws a hat and sunglasses on the pony to disguise it.

Will her disguise work?

"Uh, Emerson?" asks Kendall. "Why is that pony wearing sunglasses?"

Oops. It *didn't* work.

"Hey, wait a minute," says Willa. "That's Thunderstorm from Farmer Louie's house next door. She must have wandered over!"

"*Ohhhh.*" Emerson breathes a sigh of relief. "That makes a lot more sense. It's a pony from next door. Not a pony that someone accidentally wished for."

"Emerson, did you wish for a pony?" asks Ashlyn.

"Maybe," Emerson admits.

"You made a wish without us!" her friends cry. "How could you?"

"I was so excited," Emerson says. "But I should have waited. I'm sorry."

Emerson thinks her friends will be really angry. But instead, Camille puts her hand on Emerson's shoulder.

"I have the same problem sometimes," Camille says. "It's hard to wait when you really want something."

Ashlyn, Willa, and Kendall all nod.

"So you guys aren't mad?" Emerson asks.

"Well, we're disappointed," Willa says. "But we're not mad."

"Thanks, you guys," says Emerson. "I promise, from now on, I'll be patient."

"Then what are we waiting for?" asks Camille. "Let's go have our wishing ceremony for real!"

The friends hurry back to the well. But to their surprise, it's empty!

"Oh no! Thunderstorm must have drank all the water!" Emerson reali

Camille giggles. "It's okay. I'll bet that made the fairies laugh super hard. They'll leave us an even better wishing well next time."

Emerson grins. "And when they do, I'll definitely wait for us all to make our wish together."

"We know you will," says Ashlyn. "But just to be extra sure, maybe Camille should hold on to the coin for now?"

Emerson laughs as she hands the coin to Camille. "As you wish!"